A Note to Parents and Caregivers:

Read-it! Readers are for children who are just starting on the amazing road to reading. These beautiful books support both the acquisition of reading skills and the love of books.

The PURPLE LEVEL presents basic topics and objects using high frequency words and simple language patterns.

The RED LEVEL presents familiar topics using common words and repeating sentence patterns.

The BLUE LEVEL presents new ideas using a larger vocabulary and varied sentence structure.

The YELLOW LEVEL presents more challenging ideas, a broad vocabulary, and wide variety in sentence structure.

The GREEN LEVEL presents more complex ideas, an extended vocabulary range, and expanded language structures.

The ORANGE LEVEL presents a wide range of ideas and concepts using challenging vocabulary and complex language structures.

When sharing a book with your child, read in short stretches, pausing often to talk about the pictures. Have your child turn the pages and point to the pictures and familiar words. And be sure to reread favorite stories or parts of stories.

There is no right or wrong way to share books with children. Find time to read with your child, and pass on the legacy of literacy.

Adria F. Klein, Ph.D.
Professor Emeritus
California State University
San Bernardino, California

Editor: Christianne Jones
Designer: Amy Muehlenhardt
Page Production: Michelle Biedscheid
Art Director: Nathan Gassman
The illustrations in this book were created in watercolor and pencil.

Picture Window Books
5115 Excelsior Boulevard
Suite 232
Minneapolis, MN 55416
877-845-8392
www.picturewindowbooks.com

Printed in the United States of America.

Library of Congress Cataloging-in-Publication Data
Klein, Adria F. (Adria Fay), 1947-
Max goes to the grocery store / by Adria F. Klein ; illustrated by Mernie
Gallagher-Cole.
p. cm. — (Read-it! readers. The life of Max)
Summary: When Max and his friend Zoe want something to eat while watching
their movie, they go to the grocery store and find the ingredients for the perfect
snack.
ISBN-13: 978-1-4048-3682-2 (library binding)
ISBN-10: 1-4048-3682-9 (library binding)
[1. Grocery shopping—Fiction. 2. Friendship—Fiction. 3. Snack foods—Fiction.]
I. Gallagher-Cole, Mernie, ill. II. Title.
PZ7.K678324Mar 2007
[E]—dc22   2007004047

Max
Goes to the
Grocery Store

by Adria F. Klein
illustrated by Mernie Gallagher-Cole

Special thanks to our advisers for their expertise:

Adria F. Klein, Ph.D.
Professor Emeritus, California State University
San Bernardino, California

Susan Kesselring, M.A., Literacy Educator
Rosemount–Apple Valley–Eagan (Minnesota) School District

PICTURE WINDOW BOOKS
Minneapolis, Minnesota

Max is having his friend Zoe over to watch a movie.

Max, his mom, and Zoe go to the grocery store to buy some snacks.

Max's mom says they can each buy
two treats.

Max has an idea for a special snack.
He whispers something to Zoe.

8

She smiles and agrees.

Max picks dried fruit.

Raisins are his favorite.

Zoe picks mixed nuts.

Peanuts are her favorite.

Max picks popcorn.

14

He likes how it pops in the microwave.

Zoe picks chocolate chips.

She likes how they melt in her mouth.

Max and Zoe had fun at the grocery store.

Now they are ready to make their special snack.

Max and Zoe mix all of their treats together in a big red bowl.

Now they have trail mix.

Max picks a grape juice box. Zoe picks an orange juice box.

Max and Zoe are ready to watch
the movie.

More *Read-it!* Readers

Bright pictures and fun stories help you practice your reading skills.
Look for more books at your level.

Max Goes on the Bus

Max Goes Shopping

Max Goes to Sc hool

Max Goes to the Barber

Max Goes to the Dentist

Max Goes to the Doctor

Max Goes to the Library

Max Goes to the Playground

Max Goes to the Zoo

Max and Buddy Go to the Vet

Max and the Adoption Day Party

Max Celebrates Chinese New Year

Max Goes to a Cookout

Max Goes to the Farm

Max Learns Sign Language

Max Stays Overnight

Max's Fun Day

On the Web

FactHound offers a safe, fun way to find Web sites
related to this book. All of the sites on FactHound
have been researched by our staff.

1. Visit *www.facthound.com*

2. Type in this special code:
   1404836829

3. Click on the FETCH IT button.

Your trusty FactHound will fetch the best sites for you!

A complete list of *Read-it!* Readers is available on our Web site:

www.picturewindowbooks.com